Berlie Doherty

Illustrated by Lesley Harker

For Tommy

THE HUMMING MACHINE
A YOUNG CORGI BOOK 978 0 552 55402 2 (from January 2007)
0 552 55402 2

Published in Great Britain by Young Corgi,
an imprint of Random House Children's Books

This edition published 2006

1 3 5 7 9 10 8 6 4 2

Young Cor   ooks,
in Australia by Random House Australia (Pty) Ltd,
20 Alfred Street, Milsons Point, Sydney, NSW 2061, Australia,
in New Zealand by Random House New Zealand Ltd,
18 Poland Road, Glenfield, Auckland 10, New Zealand,
and in South Africa by Random House (Pty) Ltd,
Isle of Houghton, Corner Boundary Road & Carse O'Gowrie,
Houghton 2198, South Africa

THE RANDOM HOUSE GROUP Limited Reg. No. 954009
www.kidsatrandomhouse.co.uk

A CIP catalogue record for this book is available from the British Library.

Printed and bound in Great Britain by
Cox & Wyman Ltd, Reading, Berkshire

If Mum ... out of
their w... what

YOUNG CORGI BOOKS

Young Corgi books are perfect when you are looking for great books to read on your own. They are full of exciting stories and entertaining pictures. There are funny books, scary books, spine-tingling stories and mysterious ones. Whatever your interests you'll find something in Young Corgi to suit you: from families to football, from animals to ghosts. The books are written by some of the most famous and popular of today's children's authors, and by some of the best new talents, too.

Whether you read one chapter a night, or devour the whole book in one sitting, you'll love Young Corgi books. The more you read, the more you'll want to read!

Other Young Corgi books to get your teeth into

The Starburster by Berlie Doherty
Tilly Mint Tales by Berlie Doherty
Joe v. the Fairies by Emily Smith
Jack Slater, Monster Investigator by John Dougherty
Billy Wizard by Chris Priestley

www.berliedoherty.com

Contents

This is what happened last time:

Great-grandpa Toby gave Tam a
present. It was a kaleidoscope, but they
called it a starburster. They could see
wonderful things through it. One day,
Tam's baby sister Blue was stolen by
fairies, who left ugly goblinny Pix in
her place. Tam had to take Pix back
and find Blue again, and he had to give
the king of the fairies his starburster.

Stop That Noise

Tam was dreaming about a wonderful little tube called a starburster. When he looked through it he saw the most gorgeous shapes and colours. He had dreamed the same thing every night since midsummer's day, and he always enjoyed the dream till he got to the last bit, when he had to give the starburster away. But tonight something woke him up before he got to that bit.

Tam sat up in bed with a start. There was a terrible noise coming from somewhere. It sounded like a tin can full of bees, all buzzing at once. Or a motorbike in the bath. Or a piano being dropped downstairs – *buzz thump clang wuzz ding fuzz.*

It was awful, and it was coming from
Great-grandpa Toby's room. Tam
jumped out of bed and ran to see what
was happening. Everyone was awake
now. Mum was shouting, Baby Blue
was screaming, and Dad was
hammering on Great-grandpa Toby's
door.

"Stop that noise!" everyone shouted –
except for Blue, who stopped
screaming, took a deep breath and

screamed again, only louder.

The noise from Great-grandpa's room grew wilder and buzzier, and much worse. And now there was a kind of thumping sound too. The floor was shaking and creaking.

"You're a noisy old nuisance!" shouted Dad. "I wish you'd go and live somewhere else." He stormed off back to bed.

But the buzzing and thudding and creaking didn't stop.

Tam pushed open the door and peered in.

Great-grandpa Toby was dressed in his red stripy pyjamas. He was bouncing round the room, up and down, one step, two steps, kick, hop, jump. He was holding both his hands up to his mouth as if he was eating a sandwich. And the buzzy tin can motorbike piano noise was coming from him!

"How do you do that?" Tam shouted.
And again, "How do you do it?"

But Great-grandpa Toby had his
eyes closed and couldn't see Tam. The
noise he was making was so loud that
he couldn't hear him. And he was
jumping and kicking and hopping so
wildly that it was impossible to get
anywhere near. It was a terrible shindig
he was making.

At last he stopped. He sank down on the edge of his bed with a sigh like a vacuum cleaner that's just been switched off. His room was filled with silence. Beautiful, white, cool silence.

But Tam was still shouting, "*How do you do that?*"

He noticed that the noise had stopped.

"Great-grandpa," he whispered. "Tell me."

Great-grandpa opened his eyes and beamed at Tam. "My word, that was fun!" he said. "Look, Tam, isn't it beautiful!" He opened his hands and showed Tam a shiny silver mouth organ. "I bought it today. It's a humming machine."

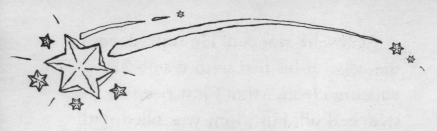

The Humming Machine

All next day Great-grandpa and Tam took it in turns to play the humming machine. Great-grandpa had to show Tam how to do it.

"Put it against your lips. Now, you suck in to make one sound, and you blow out to make another. And you slide it from side to side to do the do-ray-mi's. It's easy. As easy as breathing. As easy as humming a tune."

It made Tam's teeth feel tingly and his lips feel rubbery, and it tasted horrible, like the taste you get when you've just lost a tooth. But the noise it made inside his head was really exciting.

Dad said he'd had enough of it and was glad he was out at work all day. Mum said it gave her a headache, and she put the radio on really loud to drown out the noise. Baby Blue hated the sound at first, but she got used to it and started to gurgle and giggle whenever she heard it.

After a bit, Great-grandpa stopped sounding like a singing robot and started to be able to play real tunes. Mum even sang along with him sometimes, when she wasn't thinking.

"My word," said Great-grandpa. His lips were red with so much blowing and sucking, as if he'd been eating strawberries. "I've lived for ninety years and I've never played a humming machine before."

"You might be ninety years old," said Mum, "but you're behaving like a nine-year-old. Put that harmonica away and eat your lunch."

But as soon as Great-grandpa put it down, Tam picked it up. He got used to the tingly teeth and the wubbly lips. He got used to the tangy taste. He loved it as much as Great-grandpa did. He loved the little box it lived in when it wasn't being played at all. It had a lid that snapped shut like a crocodile's mouth, and inside it was lined with soft green velvet.

"It's the best thing ever!" he said.

"My word," said Great-grandpa Toby. "It's nearly as good as the starburster."

And Tam went quiet and sad, because really nothing, nothing in the world, was as good as his starburster. And he'd given that to the king of the fairies. He'd had the most exciting adventure of his life when he had gone to Faery to rescue Blue – but oh! how he missed his wonderful starburster!

When he went to bed that night he
was still a little bit sad. He couldn't
sleep. He was still awake when Mum
and Dad went to bed. He knew Great-
grandpa was still awake too, because he
could hear him playing his humming
machine. It wasn't his usual bright and
breezy shindig of a tune. He was
playing quietly so he wouldn't disturb
anyone, and the tune was as soft and
sad and sweet as drops of rain. Tam lay
in bed listening to it and watching how
the moon filled his room with blue
light.

Suddenly he jumped out of bed and
ran to the window.

The moon was blue!

"Remember the Sapphire Stars?"

Tam ran straight to Great-grandpa's room. He gave him such a fright that Great-grandpa nearly swallowed his humming machine.

"Great-grandpa, look! Look at the sky!" Tam shouted.

"My word!" said Great-grandpa, pulling back his curtains. "I've never seen anything like this, Tam. It's the rarest thing you can have, a blue moon. Once in a blue moon, anything can happen. Fancy, I've lived all these years and this is the first time I've seen a blue moon."

"And look at the stars! They're blue as well! And they're dancing!"

It was true. The stars were dancing
and swarming in the sky as if they were
brilliant blue bees.

"Remember the sapphire stars?" Great-grandpa asked softly.

"Of course I do," said Tam. "We saw them the night Blue was stolen by the fairies."

They looked at each other. "It had better not happen again!" they both said at the same time.

They ran into Blue's room. It was bathed in sapphire light. But Blue was still there in her cot, safe and sound. She opened her eyes sleepily and smiled at them.

"Thank goodness you're safe!" said Tam. He lifted her out of her cot with her blanket still wrapped round her to keep her warm, and hugged her tight.

"The fairies are coming, Blue. But don't be frightened. We won't let them steal you this time. Will we, Great-grandpa?"

He heard a slight whirring sound, and turned round quickly.

Great-grandpa Toby had gone.

Once in a Blue Moon

Standing just where Great-grandpa
Toby had been was a little girl with
golden-sandy-coloured skin and bright
yellow hair. She smiled proudly at Tam.

"I did it! My first job, and I got it
right, Tam."

"Who are you?" Tam asked.

The little girl sighed. "Don't you
remember me? Don't you remember me
at all?" She rolled her lips back and
pulled the ugliest, goblinniest face you
can imagine, and then smiled sweetly at
Tam again.

"You're Pix!" Tam gasped. "Pix,
you've come back! I never thought I'd
see you again!" His voice sounded

strange. He coughed and tried again.
"But what have you done with Great-
grandpa Toby?" He really did sound
odd. His voice was getting gruffer and
deeper.

Pix didn't seem to notice. "The king
of the fairies wanted to see him," she
said. "So we've — well, we've just
whisked him off to Faery. He'll be fine.
Guess what! I flew here all on my own,
Tam." She skipped round so he could
see how her shimmery wings were
folded neatly across her back.

"Great-grandpa's gone to Faery?" Tam repeated in his strange new voice. He cleared his throat to try to make the gruffness go away, but it didn't help. "But I thought only a nine-year-old boy could go there."

"Exactly," said Pix. She stopped skipping about. "I had to do a little switching job. It's worked so well! I'm so clever! No one will know the difference."

"Pix! What have you done?" With horror, Tam realized why his voice had grown so deep. He felt his chin. It was prickly with whiskers! And when he lowered Blue back into her cot, he could see that his hands were bumpy and spotty, just like Great-grandpa Toby's.

"Oh no!" His voice was growly with tears. "I know what you've done. You've turned Great-grandpa into a nine-year-old boy, and you've turned me into an old man! I'm my own great-grandpa!"

"Don't break, Tam," Pix said anxiously. "Please don't break. You're a very nice old man."

"But I don't want to be an old man.

I won't be able to play football, or ride my bike! And what will they say when I go to school? My friends will all laugh at me! They won't even know me!"

"It'll be all right, Tam. And think what a nice time your great-grandpa's having in Faery."

Tam stopped crying. "I don't believe he's gone to Faery. When I went there I had to take something silver and something velvet with me. What about those? He hasn't got anything like that."

"Oh yes he has," said Pix happily. She put her hands to her mouth and made a buzzing noise.

"His humming machine," Tam sighed. "And its velvet box. So it's true, he *has* gone, and I'll never be a young boy again." His voice was wobbling. Then he brightened up again. "Ah, I know he hasn't really gone to Faery! You can only go there on the stroke of noon on midsummer's day – and it's winter now. Midsummer's day was ages ago!"

He felt happier now. At least if Great-grandpa was tucked up in bed or hiding somewhere, there was a chance that Pix might change them back again before it was too late. But she just smiled her sweetest smile at him and hopped onto the windowsill.

"Once in a blue moon, anything can happen," she said. "Remember?"

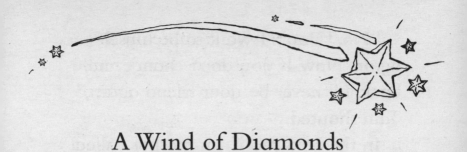

A Wind of Diamonds

"I thought you were nice, Pix. I thought you were my friend," Tam said. He was beginning to feel angry. He looked down at his wrinkled hands. "Just look what you've done to me."

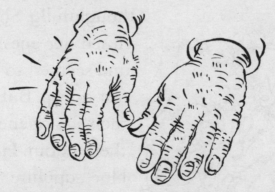

Pix stopped her ecstatic whizzing round the room and stared at Tam. "Don't you like being a very old man?" she asked, surprised.

23

"No, I don't. I want to be myself again. Now. If you don't change me back, I'll never be your friend again," Tam shouted.

In the next room, his mother called back sleepily, "All right, Grandpa?"

"See! Even Mum thinks I sound like him," Tam whispered. "Please! I love Great-grandpa Toby. But I don't want to be him. Please make me nine again."

Pix plucked a rose from the vase on the windowsill and chewed the petals

thoughtfully. She closed her eyes and seemed to fall fast asleep. But then she opened them again. Her blue, sapphire eyes stared at Tam as if she could see right through him.

He felt a strange sensation, as if his skin was being wound up tight, and a prickly, itchy feeling in his chin. He touched his face nervously. It was smooth once more. He looked down at his hands. They were soft and young. Tam's hands.

"My word," a deep voice came from Blue's cot. "I do feel strange."

Tam stared into the cot. "Now you've turned *Blue* into Great-grandpa!" he said. "Look at her whiskery face! What kind of a fairy are you?"

"Yes, what's going on?" grumbled Blue.

"Oops!" said Pix. "Not quite right!"
Tam peered anxiously at his baby
sister with her crumpled face and
watery eyes. "What's Mum going to
say?" he asked. "Pix, you're going to
have to do something about this."

"All right, all right. I'm only a
beginner, you know." She blew gently
through the bars of the baby's cot, and
something sparkled in the pale blue
moonlight, drifting down like tiny flakes
of snow.

"Aboo. Abababoo," gurgled Blue
happily. She was a baby again. She
stuck her thumb in her mouth and went
to sleep. Tam looked down and checked
his hands, just to make sure he was still
a boy.

Pix sighed with relief. "Just a little
joke! Aren't we having fun! But
someone's going to have to be an old
man, or my magic won't work. Let's see
now!"

She gazed round Blue's room, and
then stared at a big fluffy teddy bear
that was perched on a shelf.

"Aha!" she said, tapping Teddy's
threadbare paw.

"My word!" the teddy bear growled.

"That'll do," Pix said. "I don't think I
can manage more than that. Oh but
Tam, look at the moon. It's fading."

It was true. The stars were still and
silver again. The moon was slipping
down behind the rooftops, just the
palest of blues.

"Get your silver and velvet quickly!"
Pix said.

"Why?"

"I was having such a good time, I
nearly forgot. The king wants to see
you too. And I'm allowed to fly you to
Faery all by myself, because we're
friends. We are, aren't we?" she added
anxiously. "Quick, before the moon
turns white, or we'll never make it."

Tam felt a tingly rush of excitement and fear. Faery again! Last time it had been full of danger and adventure. He had seen so many wonderful things, but now it all felt as if it had been a fantastic dream. Would he really dare to go again? But it looked as if he would be going anyway, whether he wanted to or not, the way Pix rushed him about.

They ran into Tam's room and found his red dressing gown with its furry velvet collar, and then the plastic sword that he and Dad had painted grey when he was about seven. Tam remembered how the green-toothed guardian of Faery had turned his dressing gown into a cloak, and his plastic toy into a real flashing silver sword. He tried to remember the name he had given it. Winander – that was it, after the name of his road. And the guardian had changed it to a fairy name. Vinand'r.

"I won't have to use it again, will I?" he asked, worrying again. "I had to chop off the nightmares' heads with it last time."

"If you don't hurry up, *I'll* be turned into a nightmare," Pix said. "We're ready now, surely."

"Oh, wait a minute. I've just remembered something." Tam tiptoed into Blue's room and planted a kiss softly on her head, very careful not to wake her up.

"Bye, Baby Blue," he whispered. "I don't know when I'll ever see you again."

The teddy bear on the shelf growled softly.

"Bye, Teddy," Tam whispered. "Keep an eye on Blue. And don't talk too much."

He paused outside Mum and Dad's room. Dad was snoring, Mum was whistling gently in her sleep.

"Bye," he whispered. "I'll try and bring Great-grandpa home."

Then he rushed downstairs to the kitchen, picked up his green school rucksack and opened the fridge door. There was his lunch box, all neatly packed for tomorrow. He pushed it into his rucksack, and then at the last minute snatched his dad's and shoved that in too.

"Sorry, Dad, but I'm not allowed to eat any of the food in Faery," he whispered. "Anyway, all they eat is roses and buttercups."

"Now!" said Pix, dancing round with impatience. "Hold my hand."

"Do I have to?" Tam protested.

And before he could think, he felt his tummy turning circles inside him. Lights streamed and rushed and flashed. He was spinning, faster and faster, in a wind that was sparkling like crystals and diamonds. He could feel air swirling round him. He clung onto Pix's hand and laughed with joy.

If Mum and Dad had looked out of their window they'd have seen what appeared to be a brilliant blue star streaking across the sky, trailing a white spinning twist of air like a comet. They'd have heard a voice singing out, "I'm flying, Pix! I'm really flying!" and another voice shouting, "Hold on tight!"

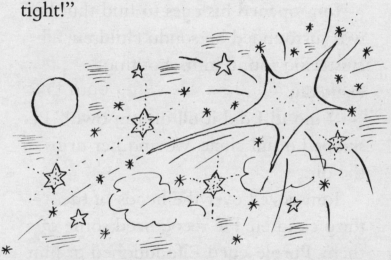

But they didn't see, and they didn't hear, because they were fast asleep.

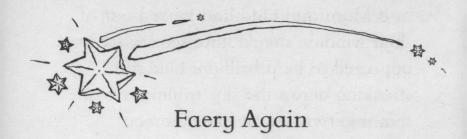

Faery Again

"Tamlin's back! Prince Tamlin's back!"

Tam opened his eyes to find that he was surrounded by sandy children, all clustering round him, shouting excitedly.

"I did it! I did it all on my own!" Pix skipped a full circle, waving her arms in the air.

Tam gazed over the heads of the fairy children. He recognized some of them. Purple-eyed Elfa laughed at him and held her fist up to her eye as if she was looking through a starburster.

"Am I really here? Am I really back in Faery?" The gorgeous colours and scents around him were so familiar that he felt as if he had never been away. "But we didn't come through the green passage! We didn't see the guardian."

"I was only a baby last time, remember," Pix said. "I didn't have wings."

She had tucked her wings across her back, but every time she turned, they flashed with the brilliant colours of dragonflies. She danced round again, so pleased with herself that she nearly bumped into a tall golden-haired woman, who came running across the grass towards them.

"Well done, Pix!" the woman said. "The king will be very pleased with you. Welcome back, Prince Tamlin!"

"You're Tanta, aren't you? I remember you!" Tam said. "You turned into a salmon when Elfa threw my starburster into the pool, and then you turned into a horse and took me over the mountains."

"I can't do that again," Tanta said sadly. "I used up all my power doing that. But never mind, it was worth it. This time you'll have to make your own way to the king, and you'll have to be quick, and very, very brave. And I warn you, he's really angry."

Pix stopped dancing. "Why?"

"Not with you, Pix. He's angry with the fairies who brought the other little boy."

"She means your great-grandpa," Pix told Tam. "Toby."

"Toby? Tobit, his fairy name will be.

Well, I'm sorry about what happened if you know him, Prince Tamlin. The fairies who did it have been turned into nightmares, of course – and don't you even think about chopping off their heads like you did last time. They deserve to be nightmares till the next blue moon."

"But why? What have they done?"

"I'm afraid something awful has happened. They've lost him."

"Lost him? Where? How?"

"I don't know," said Tanta. "That's the truth."

When she said that, a little green elf came running towards them, stumbling over his own feet in his great hurry.

"Morva see-saw!" he shouted.

"You saw what happened, Morva?" Tanta asked.

Tam recognized the little elf who had shown him the way to the king's secret tower when he was looking for Blue.

"Tobit snitch-snatched," Morva said. His eyes were bulging out of his head with excitement and fear. "Hag-dam flittered Tobit."

"Ah," said Tanta, "so that was it."

A *wheesssh* of silence fell across the fairy children. Some of them hid their faces in their hands. Morva crept up to Tam and stroked him sadly.

"What did he say?" Tam demanded.

"The Damson-hag has flown away with Tobit," said Tanta. "We'll never find him now."

Pix sank down onto the grass and hugged her knees. "Poor Tobit," she muttered. "Poor, poor Tobit."

"Please tell me who the Damson-hag is, and where she lives, and what she's going to do with my great-grandpa," Tam said.

Tanta shook her head. "I can't tell you anything. I can't speak anything about the Damson-hag. It's forbidden. It's too dangerous for me, or for any of my children here."

"But what can I do?" wailed Tam. "He's my only great-grandpa. Mum says he's an awful nuisance sometimes, and Dad wishes he would go away. He's ever so noisy. But I love him."

Morva tugged at Tanta's skirt. "Flame-reader," he whispered.

"Yes, Flame-reader!" Pix said. She jumped up and danced round Tanta again. "Flame-reader knows everything, doesn't he? We could ask him. I've never even seen him. I've always wanted to see him, Tanta. Can I go? Can I take Tam there?"

"You could try. It won't be easy." Tanta bent down and put both her hands on Tam's shoulders. "You must be very brave, Prince Tamlin. The Flame-reader is the oldest of all the fairies. He knows everything, as Pix said. But he keeps himself away from all of us."

"Morva show path," the elf said. His eyes had grown huge with fright.

"Good." Tanta nodded. "Pix and Morva will show you the way to his cave. It's through the forest of ten thousand soldier trees, that's all I know. But he hates mortals. You must wear your cloak."

Trembling, Tam opened up his

rucksack and pulled out his red dressing
gown. As he shook it out it turned into
a long velvet cloak.

"And you must use your sword."

"It's only plastic," Tam said, but as he
drew it out of his belt it flashed silver.
"Vinand'r!" he said proudly. He felt like
a real prince now.

"Nightmares will follow you, but remember to leave them behind. The king of the fairies will deal with them, not you! You must not touch them with your sword. And you must be brave. And when you meet the Flame-reader, you must not ask him any questions. Go now, quickly." And unexpectedly Tanta bent down and kissed him. It felt as soft as a butterfly touching his cheek, but it seemed to fill Tam with courage.

"I'm ready." He clutched his sword and looked round. "Come on Morva, come on Pix," he said. "Let's go."

Nightmares

Morva and Pix were so scared that they
held hands as they ran behind Tam.
Morva shouted out directions but he
wouldn't go in front, not for anything.
Far away they could hear terrifying
baying and howling, and before long
wild dogs came pounding towards
them. They had huge heads and yellow
teeth, blazing orange eyes and long
lollopy, dripping tongues. Tam knew
these were the nightmares.

They swirled around Tam and Morva
and Pix, yapping and snarling, growling
and grizzling. Poor little Morva fell
over and lay with his legs kicking the
air, and refused to go any further.

"Morva only elf," he sobbed. "Teeny tiny elf."

"All right," Tamlin said. "I won't make you come with me."

The little elf scuttled away like a rabbit. Pix jumped onto Tam's back and clung to him, trembling. "Elves are such cowards, aren't they, Tam?"

"I don't feel very brave myself," Tam said, gripping his sword. He kicked one of the dogs away, and it snapped its yellow fangs at him, drooling slimy green saliva.

"I don't like them," Pix yelled. "Use Vinand'r. Chop off their heads!"

"I want to," Tam said. "I could do that easily, and they'd turn back into fairies and everything would be all right. But Tanta said I mustn't, didn't she? It would make the king angry. Hang on tight, Pix. I'm going to run through them. I've got to, or I'll never find out where Great-grandpa is."

He could see the forest ahead of him, not far now. He closed his eyes and ran as fast as he could, ignoring the nightmares as they leaped and howled around him. He tried to keep his mind fixed on Great-grandpa Toby. And as soon as they reached the edge of the forest of ten thousand soldier trees, something strange happened. The nightmares stopped following him.

They crouched down to the ground with their ears flattened against their heads, and they started whining pitifully. One by one they began to slink away. It seemed that even they were frightened of the Flame-reader, the oldest fairy of them all.

The Forest of Ten Thousand Soldier Trees

Tam lowered Pix down and gazed helplessly at the tangled web of trees and branches and brambles in front of them. He tried to push his way forward, but the branches closed down, barring his way. Twigs snagged his hair, tree roots poked out of the ground like scabby hands, snatching at his feet.

"Is this the only way to the Flame-reader's cave?" he asked.

Pix nodded miserably. "Nobody ever goes in or out," she said.

"I'm not surprised," said Tam. "Those soldier trees will tear us to bits if we ever try to go in there." He sat down on a lumpy tree stump, nearly crying in despair. "We've been so brave. We ran all the way through that pack of nightmare dogs, and we didn't turn back. But this is hopeless. Now we'll never find Great-grandpa Toby."

"Don't break," Pix said. "You're a prince, remember."

Tam stared at her. "Prince Tamlin! Of course I am! I know how we can get through! I can use my sword!" He pulled Vinand'r out of his belt and held it high, so it flashed in the sunlight.

Then he waved it in front of him and hacked his way through the forest, slashing from left to right, round his head, round his feet, and Pix skipped behind him screaming out with delight:

"Take that, you trippy old tree! Take that, you bristly old bramble! You won't stop Prince Tamlin!"

At last they came to a massive shoulder of rock, as black as ebony. A huge hole like a yawning mouth opened up.

They had reached the cave of the Flame-reader.

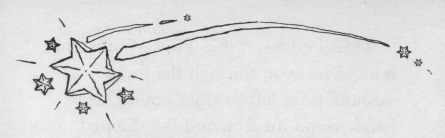

The Flame-Reader

The Flame-reader was standing in front of the cave mouth. At first Tam thought he was an ancient, bent tree. His skin was wrinkled and gnarled and grey like old wood, and his fingers and toes were like twisted twigs. His hair and beard rustled and crackled like clumps of old dry leaves. His eyes were deep, black holes, with no light in them at all.

"Who's making all that noise?" He spoke in a dry, splintery voice.

Tam took a deep breath. "I'm Tam," he said.

"Prince Tamlin," whispered Pix. She was hiding behind him. Tam could feel her trembling. He could hear her teeth chattering.

"I see by your cloak that you are
truly a prince," the crackly voice said. "I
see by your sword that you have
hacked my soldiers down."

"And are you . . . ?" Tam began, but
Pix poked him quickly.

"No questions!" she hissed.

"I mean, you are the Flame-reader."

"I am." The ancient fairy nodded, and his bones creaked, his leafy hair rustled. "What do you want?"

"Where's— Erm, no, I don't mean that. I mean, I want to know where my great-grandpa Toby is. He's very old, you see, and he shouldn't be here at all."

The Flame-reader stood still. For a long time nothing at all happened. "There are no very old mortals in Faery," the splintery voice said at last. "They simply do not come here." He turned, creaking, and began to make his way into the cave.

Pix peered out from behind Tam's back. "Please, oldest of all fairies, I turned him into a little boy.

He's called Tobit here." She dodged
back behind Tam, covering her eyes
with her fists.

The Flame-reader creaked back
round. There was a tiny glimmer in the
black holes of his eyes. "Tobit. You want
to know where Tobit is?"

"Yes, yes please," stammered Tam.

"You want me to read flames? You
want a fire?" The voice crinkled away
to nothing.

"I – yes, I think so."

To Tam's horror the Flame-reader
began pulling bits off himself and piling
them onto the floor of the cave. He
held out his right arm to Tam.

"Chop!" he said. "Chop!"

"I can't chop your arm off!" Tam
gasped.

"Chop!" the Flame-reader ordered.

"Do it, Tam," Pix whispered.

So Tam raised his sword with both
hands and it whistled sharply down

onto the Flame-reader's arm. Snap! The
arm clattered onto the floor of the cave
and broke into twigs. Tam dared himself
to look at the Flame-reader. Little green
buds were growing in his shoulder,
where the arm had been. And where he
had pulled bits off himself, tiny sprigs of
leaves were unfurling.

The Flame-reader leaned towards the
pile of twigs on the cave floor and
rubbed the twiggy fingers of his left
hand together. Smoke and then flames

curled out from the ends of his fingers.
He dropped his hand into the middle of
the stick pile and a slow, greedy fire
began to burn. But where his hand had
been, little green buds were sprouting
from his wrist.

"Fairy magic," Pix murmured.
"That's very clever."

"I thought he was going to die," Tam
whispered back.

"Fairies never die," the Flame-reader
said. His voice was sharper than before,
not nearly so old and splintery. "Watch
the flames, mortal boy. Watch, and
listen, but do not ask."

The flames were licking over the pile of wood. They flickered like coloured flies, from one colour to another, emerald and ruby, peacock, silver, peach, sunshine, every colour you would ever imagine, and they twisted and writhed into endless shapes and patterns. At last all the colours seemed to mingle together and become a hazy blue, and then just a few white wisps, and the fire died.

"What did you see?" the Flame-reader asked.

"Colours and lights," Tam said. "It was very beautiful. But what – where . . . ?" No, he mustn't ask questions, he remembered. "Oldest of all fairies, you read the flames. You know where Tobit is."

"Tobit is trapped in a golden cage. The Damson-hag has the key, and will never part with it."

Tam bit his lips and waited. He was

bursting to ask who, and why, and where, and how, but he knew he mustn't. The Flame-reader would tell him everything he wanted to know, or he would tell him nothing at all. Tam waited and waited, and at last the Flame-reader began to speak.

"Why should I tell you anything else?" he roared, his voice full and strong and young again. He pointed a bent finger at Pix, who was shivering with fright. "I have a mind to turn you into a nightmare for your part in this! Better still, as you seem to love going to mortal-land so much, I think I will make you stay there. I will turn you into a slug, and you will sit inside a daffodil trumpet for ever. Men will squeeze you and poison you and drown you, thrushes will eat you, but you will never die because you are a disgraced fairy. Every year you will be back again, another slug in another daffodil."

"But oldest of fairies, I only did what the king asked me to do," Pix pleaded.

The Flame-reader ignored her. He turned to Tam. "And as for you, I will turn you into a soldier tree. Your bones will turn to wood, your blood will turn to sap, your toes will root you to the ground."

Tam looked with horror at his feet to see if it was happening yet. He wriggled his toes fiercely. But when he looked up, he saw that the Flame-reader was laughing.

"I could do these things, but I won't.

58

You may not be a real prince, but you are as brave as anyone I have ever met. I have decided to help you instead. I will tell you the story of the Damson-hag."

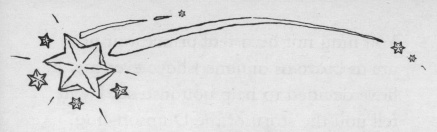

The Flame-Reader's Story

"I haven't seen the Damson-hag for thousands of years," he began. "She was once very beautiful. She has a son who is also beautiful. He is the king of the fairies."

Tam swallowed hard. So many questions were bubbling up now that he felt as if he was eating them to keep them from bursting out.

"The fairy king loves man-magic. He wanted a tube that is so magical that when you look through it the world breaks up into little pieces."

"That's my starburster!" Tam gasped.

The Flame-reader nodded. "Exactly. And now he has it, he wants a stick that sings."

"Great-grandpa's humming machine."

"And he can't have it!" the Flame-reader roared again. "We want no more of this meddling with mortals. We have our own magic here. Man-magic could destroy us. We have no need of it!"

Tam thought about all the things that were different about Faery. He thought about the colours and the brightness, the scents and sounds, everything so much clearer than anything he had ever known before. And then he thought about home — the buildings everywhere, cars and planes, litter, crowds, computers, television, mobile phones. Nothing was the same.

He thought about missiles and war, things he had seen on the television news. Was that what the Flame-reader meant? Could he see all these things when he looked into the flames?

"I know," he whispered. "It's lovely here. It's like a lovely dream."

The Flame-reader nodded. "So leave it to us." His voice was gentle now. "We don't want anything to do with mortals here. Find the boy Tobit, and take him home. The Damson-hag wants to keep him because of the magic he has brought with him. Take him away from her, and keep him away from the king of the fairies. Will you do that? Never let him come here again. Do you hear me? Do you promise?"

"Yes," said Tam, shaking again. "I promise."

"Now I will tell you where to find him. Follow the white path. Look neither over your left shoulder nor over your right shoulder. Never turn back, whatever you may hear. But when the ruby cockerel crows, look for the golden feather and keep it safe. Then follow the stinking fox. I give you Spinner to help you in your task."

He held up his hand, and a silver spider bobbed down like a yo-yo from his finger.

The Flame-reader wrapped her thread round Tam's wrist, then gave a deep sigh like the sound of wind in fir trees, and simply disappeared. His cave disappeared, and the tangled forest that surrounded it. The day disappeared and turned into hollow night. Deep, velvet blackness was all around, except for a streak of moonlight on the ground.

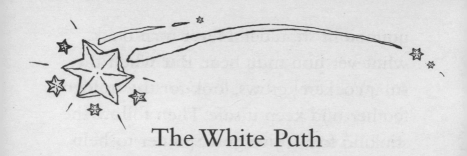

The White Path

"That was freaky!" Tam moved his hand up and down, and Spinner bobbed with him, then seemed to eat up the silver thread she had made, until she was tucked under his wrist.

"I've always wanted my very own spider," Tam said happily.

"The Flame-reader is so clever!" sighed Pix. "I can't wait till I can do that sort of magic. It takes about ten thousand years to be able to disappear."

"It's all very well for him, just going off like that, leaving us in the dark. I don't like it. What are we supposed to do now?"

"Follow the white path!" Pix jumped

up and down. "Didn't you listen? It must be this streak of moonlight."

"Well, for a start, it doesn't seem to go anywhere, just a few paces," Tam said. "And for a next, I'm starving. I'm not going anywhere till I've had a sandwich."

He sat down on the moonlight strip and took his lunch box out of his rucksack. "Do you want cheese and tomato or egg and cress?"

"I can't eat your disgusting food," Pix said. "Haven't you got any nice rosebuds in there?"

"The Flame-reader was right, you'd make a really good slug." Tam giggled.

"You'll have to make do with a bit of cress." He pulled some green stuff like strands of hair out of his sandwich and passed them to Pix. Spinner sang to herself in a high, sweet voice. "Sorry I haven't got any bluebottles for you," Tam told her. "Do you want some breadcrumbs?"

At last Tam was ready to go on. Pix insisted on having a piggyback again, as she was too tired to walk or fly. She perched on his rucksack and said she didn't mind about the lunch boxes at all, they made a nice seat. A moment later, she was fast asleep.

Tam stood in the middle of the moonlit patch and took a step forward, and then another. The path opened up in front of him as if a white carpet was being rolled away, a bit at a time, from under his feet. He walked on steadily, careful not to let his feet stray off into the darkness at either side. At first he

66

could hear nothing except the sound of
his footsteps, and sometimes a contented
snore from Pix. Spinner's tiny spidery
song spiralled around him, high and
sweet and very comforting.

Suddenly there was a shout behind
him. Tam stopped and listened. There it
came again. "Prince Tamlin! Prince
Tamlin!"

Pix was wide awake now. "Don't look round," she hissed.

But the shout came again. It sounded like the Flame-reader's voice.

"Turn, turn, that way spells danger. You've gone the wrong way. Come back. *Come back.*"

"It's not him," Pix whispered.

"It *is* him! It's his voice."

"But you mustn't look back. He said so. Remember?"

"I know," said Tam. "*Look neither over your left shoulder nor over your right shoulder*, he said. But what if he's trying to tell me I've gone the wrong way?"

"But there isn't another white path. Go on, Tam."

Tam took another step forward.

"Danger!" the voice called. "Turn back."

Tam stopped, worried.

The night was full of noise now, all kinds of noises — animal shrieks and howls, wild laughter, whisperings and moanings. The white path shrivelled under his feet and disappeared. Only darkness lay ahead.

"This way, this way," whispered the voice, smooth as a cat. It was just behind his left shoulder. "Turn this way, and you'll be safe."

"No, no, I won't go that way," Tam said firmly.

The sound came at his right side, shrieking now, wailing and angry, ten voices or more, like a yard of fighting cats.

"This way, this way."

He put his hands over his ears and shut his eyes tight. He felt himself being spun round like a leaf in the wind. Spinner crawled into his palm and tucked herself inside it, trembling. Pix put her arms round his neck and clung on, gasping for breath. At last the spinning stopped. Tam was so dizzy he could hardly stand upright. He opened his eyes slowly and waited for the world to be still again.

"Go forward, Prince Tamlin," Pix urged.

But ahead of him was complete blackness. He had no idea which way he was facing. What if the path lay in the other direction now? The voice was still swirling around him like a zizzing insect now, an annoying bluebottle. He lifted his hand as if to swish it away, and at the same time he lifted his foot to step forward. Two things happened. Spinner shot out from under his palm and strangled the insect voice as if she were eating a fly. Zzzzzgulp! It was gone. And the white path ribboned out again ahead of Tam.

He ran along the path. Whatever it was that the Flame-reader had sent to test him had been beaten and eaten. Surely nothing could go wrong.

"What else did the Flame-reader tell us, Pix?" he asked, but she was fast asleep again already.

Spinner sang softly to herself: "*Never turn back. When the ruby cockerel crows, look for the golden feather. Keep it safe. Follow the stinking fox.*" The song made a chiming beat for Tam to run to.

The darkness around them began to fade to a pearly grey. Dawn was coming. A ruby-red cockerel strutted onto the path ahead of Tam.

"*Cock-a-doodle-doo!*" It held up its crimson-crest head and crowed loudly, then clattered away again, dropping a feather as it flew. It shone like a golden arrow.

"*Pick it up! Pick it up and keep it safe!*" Tam laughed. "I remember!" He picked the feather up and stuck it in his hair. Instantly the air was filled with sunlight, and the white moon path disappeared. Little paths ran in every direction, like the tracks rabbits make in the grass.

Tam stood with his hands on his hips, gazing in despair at the maze of trails. "Now which way?"

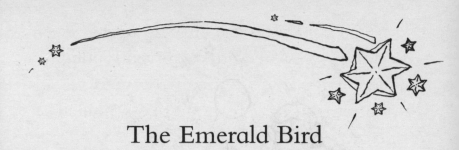

The Emerald Bird

Pix yawned sleepily, and Tam set her down on the ground.

"Which way?" she asked, rubbing her eyes. She looked up at Tam. "Oh, I like your feather."

Spinner bobbed up and down on her thread, twisting this way and that like the needle of a compass. "Which way, which way?"

Something unseen rustled in front of them, then a snake slid onto one of the tracks. It was green and gold, just the colour of sunlight on grass. It turned its head towards them.

"Thissss way," it hissed. "Ssssee me come, ssssee me go." It coiled away and was lost in the grass.

"Did the Flame-reader tell us to
follow a snake?" Tam asked.

"Yessss," came a hiss, and now they
could see it again, twisting and coiling
through the yellow and green of the
grass.

"Wait for us!" Tam shouted.

He and Pix started after it.

"No!" squealed Spinner. "Don't go that way! It's leading you astray!" and at that moment the snake twisted

towards them, its eyes as bright as jewels in its head. Its tongue streaked out and snatched Spinner from Tam's wrist.

"Oh no!" Pix shouted. "It's eaten Spinner!"

But Tam was just as quick as the snake had been. He pulled his sword out of his belt. "Vinand'r!" he shouted, and with one swipe he chopped off the snake's head.

Spinner scuttled out of the snake's mouth and up the sword, and hid herself in Tam's sleeve. The snake grew another head, but it was the head of a mouse, with a pointed nose and shivery whiskers.

"I did that!" Pix said, dancing with excitement. "Tam, I did that trick! A snake with a mouse's head! Whee!"

The snake squeaked and twisted away quickly.

"Whee! Whee! Follow me!" a high birdsong voice twittered. Now a bird with wings the colour of emeralds flashed around them. Tam could feel his hair lifting with the wind it made as it fluttered round his head. It soared away from them. "Follow me!"

"How can we follow a bird?" he asked. "It's flying too fast!"

Way up in the sky, the emerald bird dipped and flashed its wings.

Pix unfurled her own wings and fluttered them prettily. "I can do that. Hold my hand, Tam."

"But it's flying so high." Tam shielded his eyes and peered up at the bird. "Wait a minute!" he shouted. "It's stolen my feather!"

Sure enough, they could see something golden and shiny in the bird's beak.

"I'll get it back!" Pix said. She spread out her wings and soared up like the bird, over Tam's head, higher and higher, swooping and circling and laughing out loud just for the fun of it. Tam shielded his eyes with his hand and watched helplessly. He saw Pix closing in on the emerald bird, faster and faster. Then the bird turned and flapped its wings at Pix. They seemed to be fighting in mid-air, tossing this way and that way like coloured rags on a washing line.

"Pix, Pix, be careful!" Tam called.

One of them broke away from the other. Because the sun was so bright behind them it was impossible for Tam to see which one was which, bird or Pix. One flew away, and one fell, spinning at first, and then dropping like a stone out of the sky.

It was Pix.

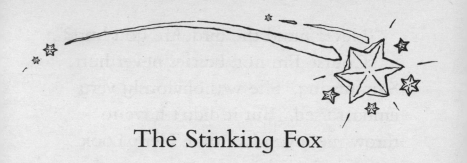

The Stinking Fox

"Pix, oh Pix!" Tam ran to where she lay stretched out on the ground. "Pix, are you all right?"

To his great relief Pix sat up and shook her wings crossly. They looked very untidy now, a bit tattered and covered with dust. "Stupid floppy old bird," she muttered.

"Never mind the bird. Are you hurt?"

"Course I'm not. Fairies never hurt. Stop fussing." She was obviously very embarrassed. "But it didn't have to throw me away like that. Here. Look after it this time."

She held out the golden feather.

"Pix, you're perfect!" Tam told her. He tucked the feather into his belt, next to Vinand'r. "I was just worried. I don't know what I'd do without you. You're my best friend."

"Am I, Tam?" She beamed happily at him and folded her wings away. "That's all right then. Now, what were we doing?"

"We were trying to find the way," Tam reminded her. "We shouldn't have followed the snake or the bird. Oh, I wish I could remember what the Flame-reader told us next. Follow the white path. We did that. Look neither over the right shoulder nor over the left shoulder. Did that. Found the golden feather. But then? Oh, wait a minute—!" He stepped forward and sniffed, then held his nose. "There's something very smelly round here." He was aware of a strong, sharp smell. "Fox!" he shouted. "That was the next thing. Follow the stinking fox!"

And now they could see it, streaking ahead of them like a tongue of flame, an orange flicker in the long grass. They ran after it, darting backwards and forwards just as the fox was doing. Once it crouched down and turned its head towards them, panting.

"We're not hunting you, mister smelly fox," Tam shouted. "We're following you."

The fox opened his mouth and laughed, and set off again.

And then, very faint, very far away, came the sound of music. It was soft and sad and low. The more they followed the stinking fox, the louder it grew. It was a buzzy sort of music, a bees-in-a-jar-of-honey sort of music. There was no mistaking the sound.

"That's Great-grandpa Toby's humming machine," said Tam. "We've found him!"

The Boy Tobit

Now they could see a large golden
cage dangling from a tree. It was
rocking gently backwards and forwards,
pushed by a sleepy old midnight-blue
bear. Inside the cage sat a boy of about
nine. His head was bowed down and his
legs were crossed. He was playing a
harmonica. The tune he was playing
was so sad that it was almost like
crying.

"It's him, it's Tobit!" squealed Pix
excitedly. "I did it! I did it! I found him,
all by myself!"

"No, you didn't," said Tam. "And
anyway, that's not Great-grandpa Toby.
That's just a boy."

The boy in the cage stopped playing
and looked up. "My word!" he said. "It's
Tam! How did you get here?"

Tam couldn't stop staring at the boy.
It was just as if he was looking at
himself in a mirror – the same untidy
hair, the same brown eyes. He suddenly
realized that the boy in the cage *was*
Great-grandpa Toby, just as he must
have looked when he was only nine
years old. He went right up to the cage

and shook the bars. The door was firmly locked.

"I'll get you out," he promised. "Oh, poor Great-grandpa!" He turned to Pix. "This is all your fault. Can't you do something to help him?"

He heard the sound of cackly laughter, and turned to see a woman coming towards them. She was very bent and ugly, with long, straggly, tangled seaweed hair and dark purple rings round her eyes. From her red sash hung a key, surely the key to the cage.

"Another mortal child!" she said in her crackly voice. "How lucky I am! And you have a fairy child with you." She scratched Pix's chin with her crooked nails. "Do you really expect *her* to break my enchantment? Mine, the queen of all queens?" and then she cooed sweetly. "Tobit is my own darling, my little hummingbird. Aren't you, my sweet?" she purred. "Sing for me, my precious."

Great-grandpa Toby put the harmonica to his mouth and played a lovely lilting tune, and the Damson-hag hobbled about in a stooped, stiff-legged dance. But as she danced something strange happened to her. Her movements became light and graceful, willowy as a young girl's. Her face grew young, her eyes shone, and were the rich colour of plums. Her matted hair became smooth and shining, swaying around her like a beautiful shimmering purple cloak.

"Mine, mine, mine," she sang. "You're my own darling hummingbird."

Tam couldn't take his eyes off her. He had never seen anyone more beautiful, or more frightening. As she danced, her shadow danced with her, a deep purple-red. It was as if there were two of her, swaying and dancing around him, laughing, while the harmonica played on.

"Dance with me, boy, dance with me!" She took hold of Tam's hands. Her fingers were icy cold. He found that he couldn't stand still. His feet were moving in time to the music. The midnight-blue bear stood up on his hind legs and rocked the cage, his huge paws padding up and down gracefully. He rumbled the tune in a deep growly voice.

"That's it, my bear pet, sing for me." The Damson-hag laughed.

And underneath the sound of her laughter and the bear's deep rumbling growl came another sound, breathy and wheezy and hardly heard, a strange, tinny song to the dancing tune:

"With golden needle and silver thread
Capture a queen in a silken web . . ."

someone seemed to be singing, very softly. It was almost as if the words were coming from the humming machine itself. It was obvious that the Damson-

hag hadn't heard it. She swung Tam
round and then, suddenly bored, let go
of his hands. She snapped her fingers
and stopped dancing. The music
stopped instantly.

"Don't think you can take my
hummingbird away from me," she
snapped at Tam. "He's mine for ever."

She tipped the cage with her fingers
so it began to rock again. "Carry on,
bear," she hissed sharply. "Do your job.
Or we'll get this nice boy to do it for
you. I'm sure he'd like to stay here too."

She waltzed away, laughing, and as
she entered the darkness of the trees her
voice grew old and cracked again, her
figure stooped, her hair straggly and
wild. "In fact," she cackled, "he won't be
leaving for a long, long time. He's mine
now. Mine! You're all mine! Every one
of you!"

"You're All Mine!"

"My word," said Great-grandpa Toby. "It's very cramped in this cage. I could do with stretching my legs a bit."

Tam tried the door again. "It's no good, I can't open it."

Pix pulled at his arm. "Come away, Price Tamlin. You heard what she said. Get away while we have the chance."

"Not without my great-grandpa," said Tam firmly.

"But how can we take him? She's got the key."

"I know." Tam nodded, frowning. "I saw it when she was dancing."

"She's very good at dancing, isn't she?" Great-grandpa sighed. "She's so kind, and so beautiful."

"She is beautiful, isn't she?" Tam agreed. "But she's so ugly too! I don't know how she does that."

"My music does it," said Great-grandpa proudly. "My music makes her as beautiful as she was when she was young. That's why I'm here, she says. I'm so happy."

Tam gasped with surprise. "Don't you *mind* being here?"

"Well, I'm a bit stiff, and I'm very hungry, but apart from that, no. I'm very lucky, having her to look at all day. She always looks beautiful to me now."

"She's enchanted him," said Pix. "Very clever, I must say."

"Starving hungry," Great-grandpa went on. "I've just about had enough of those petals she keeps giving me. Not enough for a spider to eat, they aren't. Oh, you've got one, I see."

Spinner bobbed down from Tam's

wrist and scuttled up and down the
bars of the cage.

"That's how she's done it, giving you
fairy food," Pix told him. "Don't you
eat any more of those flowers — and
don't you touch them either, Prince
Tamlin. Save them for me. She's nearly
enchanted you already, making you
dance with her like that."

"But she is very beautiful," Tam
sighed.

"There! I knew it," Pix said. "You're
going to have to be very careful, or
she'll be putting you in a cage next."

"Was that thunder, or was it my
tummy rumbling?" Great-grandpa
asked.

"Just a minute. At least I can give
you something to eat." Tam opened up
his rucksack and took out his dad's
lunch box. "I brought something for
you. I think it's Stilton cheese and onion
sandwiches. Very smelly anyway. What
a pong! Just like your socks, Great-
grandpa − I mean, when you *were* a
great-grandpa."

"Just the job!" Great-grandpa Toby
stretched his hands out between the
bars of the cage and munched
cheerfully.

"You might *feel* happy here," Tam said. "But you didn't *sound* happy when we arrived. You were playing such a sad tune."

"Oh, the humming machine just seems to play what it wants to play." It was hard to hear what he was saying with his mouth full.

Tam stared at him. "You mean, when you were playing just now, it was really the humming machine making the music?"

Great-grandpa nodded happily. "I just suck and blow, suck and blow, and out comes the music. My word, I bet you thought I was a wonderful player!"

"But what about the song? It was singing words. Real words — and it wasn't you doing it?"

Great-grandpa shook his head.

"It was telling us something!" Pix said. "Remember what it said, Tam?"

Tam frowned. "Something golden,

something silver . . ." He sighed. "No. I can't remember. See if it will sing again."

Great-grandpa picked up the harmonica and blew and sucked. Not a sound came out of it. "Hope I haven't got crumbs in it," he said anxiously.

"Something about capturing a queen . . ." muttered Pix. They stared at each other. "Try to remember, Tam."

The midnight bear stopped rocking the cage and rumbled to himself. Spinner stood with two of her arms folded.

*"With golden needle
and silver thread
Capture a queen in a
silken web . . ."*

she sang in her tiny,
high-pitched voice.

"My word!" said Great-grandpa.
"What a clever spider."

But Pix was leaping around in great
excitement. "I did it! I did it! I did it all
on my—"

"Shush," said Tam. "We haven't done
it yet."

They could see the Damson-hag
coming back towards them, stooping
stiffly every now and again to pick
flowers.

"Quick! She's coming," Tam said. "A
golden needle – where can I get one?"

"How is my precious hummingbird?"
the Damson-hag croaked. "I've brought
you a feast, my darling. Rose petals,

pink and white and red. And some for
your dear little friend. My pretty little
dancing boy."

"A needle, a needle," Tam whispered.
"Quick, someone, or she'll trap us all."

Pix jumped up and plucked the
cockerel feather out of Tam's belt.

"There!" she said triumphantly.

"Pix, you're fantastic!" Tam knelt
down and put the feather on the
ground. With the point
of his sword he
carefully pierced a hole
in the stem of the
feather. He held it up.
"A golden needle!" he
said triumphantly.

The bear growled.

"And a lily full of nectar for you all
to drink," the Damson-hag purred. She
had almost reached the cage.

"Silver thread?" Tam whispered.
"Quick!"

Spinner yodelled and swung down. Her thread spiralled behind her. Pix threaded one end through the hole in the feather. Spinner dangled upside down, spinning more thread as fast as she could.

"Quick, oh quick, oh quick!" said Pix. "Give me the needle, Tam."

"Little games?" laughed the Damson-hag sweetly. Then she kicked out viciously at Pix. "Out of my way, fairy flea."

At first she couldn't understand what Pix was doing, or why she was jumping around her so excitedly, running backwards and forwards with a feather in her hand and a spider bobbing behind her. She tried to kick her away again, then realized that her legs wouldn't move. She was bound tight, tight, in the web that Pix was sewing round her.

"Let me go!" she roared.

Her ankles were sewn together, then her fingers, then her hands. It was the magic sent by the Flame-reader, and it was stronger than anything she could do. It was powerful and completely unbreakable.

"Get me out of here! Let me go!" she screamed. "I'll turn you into scratchy cats! I'll turn your bones to jelly! I'll make you hop like frogs! I'll give you fishy fins! I'll – I'll – I'll—"

Tam ran towards her and pulled at the key that dangled from her red sash.

With one strike of his sword he  slashed the sash and the key fell into his hand.

He dashed to the cage and unlocked the door, and Great-grandpa tumbled out.

"Come on!" Tam shouted. "Leave her like that! She can't harm us now."

"I'll plague you with ants, I'll blister your feet, I'll . . ." and then there was nothing more the Damson-hag could say, because Pix sewed up her mouth.

They were free.

The Midnight Bear

They had no idea which way to run. Pix wasn't very good at running because her legs were so short. She opened her wings and fluttered them so her feet lifted off the ground every now and again. But no matter how fast they ran or flew, they could hear the sound of heavy feet lumbering after them. Pix glanced over her shoulder.

"It's the midnight bear," she panted. "We'll have to run very fast to get away from him. I could fly one of you, if you hold my hand. But I can't fly two."

Great-grandpa Toby tripped and fell over. "Go on without me," he panted.

"No way!" Tam said. "He won't

harm us, Great-grandpa. I won't let
him." He drew out his sword and flashed
it above his head. "Vinand'r!" he shouted.

"My word!" Great-grandpa said.
"You couldn't really kill a bear, could
you?"

"Of course he could!" said Pix. "At it,
Sir Tamlin! Swipe his head off!"

But Tam knew he wouldn't do it. His
hands were shaking and his mouth was
as dry as paper. "Go away, Midnight
Bear!" he tried to shout, but his voice
came out as thin as a mouse-squeak,
and the great blue-black bear lumbered
towards them. Then it stopped and
reared up on his great back legs.

"Nix bad bear!" he rumbled, and he
held out his paw towards Tam.
Dangling from it was the golden key.
"For Prince."

"What do I want that for?" Tam
asked, lowering his sword. He took the
key carefully from the bear.

The bear rubbed his paws together,
then he mimed lifting something up,
putting it inside something, closing a
door, and turning a key in a lock.

"Haggy," he chuckled deep in his
throat. "Haggy-house!" He broke out
into loud roars of laughter.

Pix was the only one to understand him. "You've put the Damson-hag in the cage, and locked it?" she asked.

The midnight bear laughed, still chuckling, and beat his chest with his paws in triumph.

Tam put his sword away. "Then you'd better come with us," he said.

So there were five of them: Tam and Great-grandpa, Pix and the midnight bear, and little bobbing Spinner, and they still had no idea where they were going, or why. But the way itself seemed clear enough, because stretching ahead was an avenue of flowers, opening up to them as they walked; every colour you could dream of, and more. The scent was rich and sweet. As they walked, Pix plucked petals and nibbled them, and every now and then the midnight bear stooped and helped himself to a handful.

"Are you really a bear?" Tam asked.

"I'm sure they eat more than that."

"Haggy-wist," he grumbled.

"The Damson-hag enchanted him," Pix translated. "He's really an elf, I think. He speaks Old Faery. Only elves talk it these days."

"Can't you turn him back?"

"Break the Damson-hag's enchantment!" Pix's eyes were wide with fear. "I can't do that! I'm only a childling. *You* must do it."

"How? I don't know any magic."

"You'll find a way, Prince Tamlin."

Tam sighed. "I don't know how to do it. And I don't know how to get Great-grandpa Toby home. I promised the Flame-reader I'd do it. *Find the boy Tobit, and take him home*, he told me."

"Well," Pix murmured uncomfortably, "I don't think that's going to be possible. Can you hear anything, Tam?"

There was a distant sound of

galloping hooves and jingling harnesses, the flapping of banners, shouts and cries, growing steadily closer. Suddenly they were surrounded by prancing horses, black, white, silver, green, deep ocean-blue, and riding them were knights dressed in black velvet. And watching them from one side were two figures that Tam recognized. One was dressed all in white, with white hair like a crown of dandelion fluff. The other had a long gown as blue as the sky, and hair like a drift of white snow.

The king and queen of the fairies.

Fairy Bargains

"At last," said the king, dismounting from his horse. "My childhood friend."

He walked straight up to Great-grandpa Toby and held out both of his hands. "Welcome! Welcome to Faery, young Tobit, prince of mortals. Welcome to the land of King Oban and Queen Tania."

"My word," said Great-grandpa. "My word." He hadn't any more words to say, because he was so amazed, and happy, and frightened, all at the same time.

"And welcome back, Prince Tamlin."

Tam bowed. He glanced nervously at the queen of the fairies, not knowing whether he should bow to her or kiss her hand or what, but the queen seemed far more interested in Great-grandpa Toby. They all did, in fact. The knights were jostling each other to get a better look at him, as if he were a pop star or something. The king was still holding both of Great-grandpa's hands, smiling at him as if he were his long-lost brother.

"We met so long ago, and here we are again after all these years – and you're still a boy and I'm still a king!"

"I'm over ninety really," Great-grandpa chuckled.

"I still have your magic seeing stick," King Oban said, "that Prince Tamlin gave me in exchange for his sister. It is a wonderful thing indeed, but it doesn't work properly." He let go of Great-grandpa at last and produced the kaleidoscope.

"My starburster!" said Tam.

"You look," said the king of the
fairies. "You mend it."

He gave it to Great-grandpa Toby,
who peered through it, twisting it this
way and that, chuckling in amazement.

"My word! I've never seen it behave
like this!"

King Oban stamped his foot. "The
colours are wishy-washy!" he grumbled.
"They're old and broken!"

Great-grandpa took the starburster
away from his eye and gazed around at
the dazzling colours of the flowers
everywhere. He looked through the
starburster again and then took it away
from his eye.

"You're right," he said. "It's because

the colours here are so very, very beautiful and dazzling that they can't get any better. So when you look through the starburster they look paler than they really are, and you see them in little pieces instead of whole and lovely. In my land, it makes the flowers glow like fairy flowers. My word" – he twisted the starburster again and smiled – "it works very differently here. It doesn't do this where I come from."

The king stamped his foot again. "Mend it!" he shouted.

"I can't," Great-grandpa said. "It's not broken, you see. It just works differently here."

"I'll have it back then," said Tam, stretching out his hand for it.

"Oh no," said the king. He took the starburster away from Great-grandpa and folded his arms. "A gift for a gift. I give you the seeing stick if you give me the singing stick."

"The singing stick?" Great-grandpa repeated. "Ah! You mean my humming machine!" He frowned. "But it's my special thing. It makes me happy when I'm sad, and it makes me dream, and it makes people dance. It's my special thing."

"Give it!" the king ordered. Reluctantly Great-grandpa took the little silver box out of his pocket. He opened it and stroked the velvet lining, then took out the harmonica and snapped the box shut.

"Play it," the king said. "Here, Prince."

He tossed the starburster to Tam, who hugged it as if he could never let it go.

He turned away from the king and looked down it, and saw something so wonderful and beautiful that he wanted to cry, something that he never thought he would see again. He could see a garden with a scruffy lawn and pale yellow flowers. He could see an old apple tree. He knew that tree. He knew that garden. He swivelled the starburster round a bit, so he was looking through the window of a house into a room. There was a baby's cot, and in the cot, his own little sister, Baby Blue, smiling as if she could see him.

Then Great-grandpa began to play his humming machine. He played the happy dancing tune that he used to play at home. Tam swivelled the starburster again, and saw Mum coming into the room. She stooped down and lifted Blue out of her cot, and started dancing around the room with her. It was as if she could *hear* the tune.

Tam looked up and saw that
everyone around him was dancing too
– the king and queen, the midnight-
blue bear, Pix, everyone, arms in the air,
faces full of laughter. Even the horses
carrying the knights were shifting their
hooves up and down in time to the
music. Great-grandpa stopped playing
and the king held out his hand.

"Mine now," he said.

Great-grandpa risked a wink at Tam, and Tam knew then that he had seen what Tam had seen when he looked through the starburster. He turned back to the king.

"Ah no," he said. "A gift for a gift. I give you my humming machine if you take the enchantment away from the midnight bear."

There was a gasp of surprise from everyone. Pix pulled a face at Great-grandpa and shook her head. One of the knights jerked his horse forward and leaned down to grab the harmonica out of Great-grandpa Toby's hand. But the king raised his hand and the knight trotted his horse back a pace or two.

"Well, Tobit. So you have learned quickly about fairy bargaining." King Oban's smile turned to anger. "I didn't place the enchantment on the bear in the first place. You want me to meddle with someone else's magic?"

"I do," said Tam's brave little great-grandpa. His knees were knocking together, but he held the humming machine tightly in his hand behind his back. "If you know how to, that is," he added daringly.

"I know how to!" the king roared. "I need to think, that's all."

He went over to the midnight bear, who started mumbling anxiously to himself. "Lixen bear offright."

"He said he quite likes being a bear really," Pix whispered to Tam. "But I think he's just scared, don't you?"

King Oban stared into the bear's eyes. Then he turned to Great-grandpa. "If I take away the bear's enchantment for *ever*, I will make one last bargain with you. Do you agree?"

"Well, what is it?" Great-grandpa asked nervously.

"Ah, I'll tell you that when I change the bear back. Agree or not? If you don't agree, he turns back into a bear every night."

"All right. I agree."

"First, the humming machine." King Oban held out his hand, and Great-grandpa Tobit tossed the harmonica across to him. The king put it to his mouth and blew a growly, nasty tune on it. He shook it and frowned and tried again. Nothing but tinny ugliness.

"You'll soon pick it up," Tam promised him. "I did. But what about the bear?"

"Oh, the stupid bear," the king snapped moodily. He clicked his tongue three times and started to play the humming machine again. This time the midnight bear started dancing, though it wasn't much of a tune and it wasn't much of a dance, but it was as if he just couldn't help himself. He turned round and round, stamping his feet crazily, and the moment the music stopped he

did a backward somersault and turned
into a green elf.

"Morva!" Tam gasped. "It was you
all the time! How did you get turned
into a bear?"

"Morva haggy-plix-plee savio Tobit,"
the little elf gabbled. "Stead haggy-wist
biggybluey bear."

"My word," said Great-grandpa.
"What was all that about?"

"Ssh!" whispered Pix. "Don't let the
king hear. He said he went to the
Damson-hag to try to rescue Tobit, but
she turned him into a bear instead."

"Well, he was a very brave elf to try,"
Tam whispered.

Morva chuckled with pride.

The king interrupted them. "Now,
Tobit, I have one last bargain to make,
and there will be no more between us.
My gift for your gift for my gift for
your gift is this: I took away the bear's
enchantment. Now you must ride on
my horse."

Great-grandpa's eyes shone. To ride on that beautiful silver-white horse, with its golden mane and tail and its reins all crusted with jewels! Why would the king want him to do that?

"No!" Tam said suddenly. "Don't do it!" and so did Pix, and so did Spinner in her tiny spirally voice, and so did Morva the elf. They all said it at the same time.

But Great-grandpa, silly little nine-year-old boy Great-grandpa Toby said, "Yes! Oh, yes *please!*"

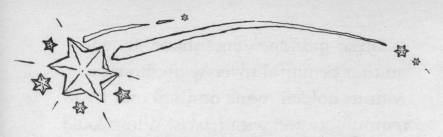

The King of the Fairies

The king signalled to one of the knights to raise the stirrups of his horse so a child could ride it.

"Tobit!" he called at last. "We are ready!"

At first it was hard to understand what was happening. Great-grandpa grinned excitedly at Tam and walked up to the towering silver horse. Then the king took off his own gleaming white cloak and flung it round Great-grandpa's shoulders. The knights cheered and roared and threw handfuls of glittering stars into the air, and the stars bloomed silver trails like fireworks. Great-grandpa was lifted high, high up

onto the saddle of the horse. The queen
trotted her sky-blue horse up to join his.

And the king went down on his
knees.

At last Tam was able to make out
what everyone was shouting.

"Hail! Hail the new king!"

"Pix? What does it mean?" he asked.

But Pix was dancing up and down, waving her arms and shouting with all the others. "Hail, King Tobit! King of the fairies!" she was shouting.

Tam ran forward, but the knights barred his way with their horses. King Tobit laughed joyfully down at him. He looked as if he would burst with pride.

"Do you hear that, Tam! King of the fairies! That's me!"

"And I am Oban again, at last!" the dandelion-headed king-that-used-to-be sighed, such a deep, deep sigh of pleasure that it was obvious that this was what he had wanted all the time.

The chief knight blew a sapphire horn, and they galloped away, all the black velvet knights, all the blue and scarlet and ruby horses, Pix and Morva and all, away they went, leaving Tam alone.

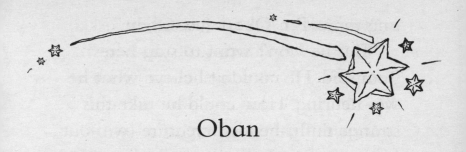

Oban

"Well, Prince Tamlin. There's just us now."

Tam turned to see that the fairy who used to be king was still there, smiling at him.

"It's just a joke, isn't it?" Tam asked. "He'll be coming back soon, won't he? And then I can take him home."

"Not a joke," Oban replied. "He's taken my place. Oh no, he's not going home. But I am."

"What do you mean?"

"I'm coming to the land of mortals." The fairy clapped his hands with joy. "I'm coming home with you! It's what I've always wanted. I'm not the king any more. I'm Oban. Just Oban."

"But he won't want to stay here," Tam said. He couldn't believe what he was hearing. How could he take this strange fluffy-headed creature (without his magnificent robe he looked more like a dandelion than ever) home with him? What would Mum and Dad say?

"You'll hate our food," he muttered.

"Puff! I can eat your garden," Oban said. "Pix told me you have roses and all sorts of flowers there."

"Not in winter. And Mum won't like it if you eat her roses. And anyway, what's Great—"

"King Tobit."

"All right, King Tobit, what's he going to eat?"

"Is that all you think about? Food?"

"Mostly," Tam admitted. His tummy was rumbling even as he spoke.

"Then stop being selfish," Oban said. "A fairy eats fairy food. Your great-grandpa has wanted to come here all his life, ever since he stood outside the green passage and knew it led to Faery; ever since he and I met when he was really nine years old. This is the best thing that's ever happened to him. This is what he has always dreamed about. Why take it away from him?"

Tam remembered Great-grandpa's face when he climbed up onto King Oban's horse, with the white robe gleaming round his shoulders. He had looked more excited and happy than anyone Tam had ever seen. And at home he was often sad because he couldn't do this and couldn't do that any more, couldn't climb trees, couldn't play football, couldn't bend to tie his shoelaces. Maybe he wouldn't get any older in Faery. Maybe he wouldn't die.

"Now," said Oban. "I'm ready to go, aren't you?" He puffed and blew on the humming machine, making awful noises. "The green passage is over that glass hill. We'll get there very soon."

Tam realized that all the time he had been thinking, they had been walking away from the spot where he had last seen King Tobit.

"I'll see so much man-magic," Oban kept sighing. "Pix has told me about the box that you keep little people in, and they sing and dance and talk whenever you want them to."

"What?" Tam frowned. Then he

grinned. "Oh, that! It's called television. It's not that good really."

"And you can talk to people when they're somewhere else, with a little stick that you keep in your pocket."

"Mobile phones. Mum said I can have one when I'm older." Tam was beginning to cheer up. After all, he was going home. He was going to see Mum and Dad and Blue again. And it would be quite fun to show Oban all these gadgets. What would he make of his bike? he wondered. And aeroplanes, and cars?

"Mobile phones! We should have things like that here," Oban chuckled. "Such wonderful magic!"

Tam remembered what the Flame-reader had said. *We want no more of this meddling with mortals. We have our own magic here. Man-magic could destroy us. We have no need of it!*

"No, you'd ruin it!"

"Why? Why shouldn't we have it?" Oban demanded.

"Because . . . because . . ." It was so hard to explain. "Because what you've got is better. And we can never have it where I live, not your kind of magic, not dream magic." Because that was what it was. It didn't seem real any more. Nothing seemed real. And the words of the flame-reader were chiming in his ears:

Find the boy Tobit, and take him home. Will you do that? Never let him come here again. Do you hear me? Do you promise?

But how could he keep his promise? He had found Tobit and lost him again, because of fairy trickery. He didn't know how to play tricks like that.

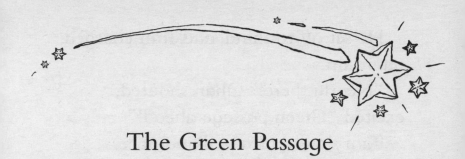

The Green Passage

The last bit of the journey was an exciting slippery scramble up one side of the glass mountain and a top-speed slide down the other. They were both shouting their heads off when they reached the bottom.

"Amazing!" Oban laughed. "You just can't do that when you're a king." He turned to Tam. "Aren't we having fun together! Race you!"

He set off running, and Tam charged after him.

"Nearly there!" Oban shouted, excited. "Green passage ahead!"

Tam slowed to a walking pace.

They were approaching the misty darkness of the cave that led to the green passage and home. He felt a lump in his throat. He hadn't said goodbye. He would never see his great-grandpa again, and he had never even said goodbye. When they entered the gloom of the cave they could just see a tiny pinprick of blue light at the far end. Tam knew it was the light of home.

The guardian of the cave came stumbling towards them, green-toothed and grinning, rubbing his cracking fingers together.

"Snix snee," he cackled, recognizing Oban. "Kingy-bye?"

"Yes, I'm going." Oban smiled. "King

Tobit will take care of you all now."

Then Tam saw shapes moving in the
darkness as all the sleeping soldiers
woke up and stretched and struggled to
their feet to salute the departing king.
Their long grey beards touched the

ground. It was the first time they had been awake for a thousand years, and their limbs were stiff and their old eyes blinked sleepily. They peered at Oban, trying to recognize him without his magnificent cloak.

"Seven more steps, and we'll be there!" Oban laughed.

Tam had never felt more miserable in his life. He put his hand in his pocket and felt his starburster. He put it to his eye and looked around. The blue light that showed through the crack in the boulders sparkled like jewels. He twisted the starburster round and now he could see the secret bower where the king and queen of Faery lived. He could see the queen sleeping in her hammock as it swayed gently backwards and forwards.

He moved the starburster again. He could see Morva and Pix, munching petals. And now, at last, he saw a little boy in a dazzling white cloak. He was sitting cross-legged on a throne. Elfa, the pretty fairy with purple eyes, was hovering round him with bowls overflowing with petals. The boy looked up for a moment. His eyes were shining. He gazed straight at the starburster as if he knew he was being watched. His lips moved, and although Tam couldn't hear a word of it he knew what Great-grandpa Toby was saying.

"Goodbye, Tam."

He put the starburster back in his pocket.

"Ready?" Oban asked.

"Ready," said Tam.

Together they put out their hands and touched the mossy green boulders. With no effort from them at all, the boulders swung apart. The brilliant blue of day rushed to meet them. They stepped forward and the boulders slid together behind them without a sound.

They were home.

Tilly Mint Tales
Berlie Doherty

Mrs Hardcastle was fast asleep.
And Tilly Mint was bored . . .

When Tilly's mum goes out to
work, Mrs Hardcastle from up the
street pops in to look after her.
There are two special things about Mrs Hardcastle. The
first thing is that she's always dropping off to sleep (she
snores too, sometimes). The second special thing is that
whenever she goes to sleep, something magic always
seems to happen to Tilly Mint!

Carnegie-Medal-winner Berlie Doherty's enchanting
Tilly Mint tales are at last available in one complete
collection.

'Full of affection and good humour.'
Times Literary Supplement

'Children will warm to the comforting and
comfortable figure of Mrs Hardcastle' *TES*

Young Corgi 0 552 54870 7